Purple Ronnie's History of the World

First published 1999 by Boxtree
an imprint of Macmillan Publishers Ltd
25 Eccleston Place London SW1W 9NF
Basingstoke and Oxford

www.macmillan.co.uk

Associated companies throughout the world

ISBN 0 7522 17313

9 8 7 6 5 4 3 2 1

A CIP catalogue record for this book is
available from the British Library

Text by Giles Andreae
Illustrations by Janet Cronin
Printed and bound in the EC

Contents

 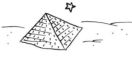
 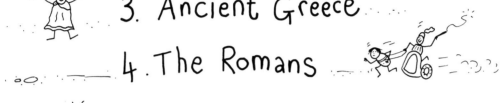

CAVE MEN

a poem about
Cave Men

Cave Men who wanted a girlfriend
Didn't know how to behave
Instead of a candle-lit dinner
They'd just drag one home to their
cave

History

A very very very long time ago there was an enormous Bang in Space and suddenly the World was made

At first there were no people at all—just dinosaurs. But one day it got very cold and all the dinosaurs died because they hadn't invented thermal undies yet

When the sun came out again, people who looked like monkeys began crawling out of the slime

Soon the monkey people started to look more like Human Beings and that is how Cave Men began

What Were Cave Men Like?

Looks

Cave Men had long hair, huge muscles and hairy backs- so did Cave Women

Cave Men

Because they still hadn't invented clothes, Cave Men used to run around with their Dangly Bits wobbling all over the place

Cave Women

The main thing about Cave Women is that they had incredibly floppy bosoms

At first, Cave Men did not know how to speak, so they spent a lot of time just grunting at each other

What Did Cave Men Do?

Cave Men spent their whole time chasing after wild animals

Cave Women used to gather berries or hang out by the fire gossiping about their boyfriends

What Did Cave Men Believe In?

Cave Men did not have any gods but they did like to worship the sun and the moon

Instead of praying, Cave Men built huge rings of stones where they would have naked hippy discos in the middle of the night

Contributions to the World

The most brilliant invention that Cave Men made was the Stick Man. They used to paint them all over the walls of their houses

Cave Men also invented fire which is something we still use today

Cooking was thought up by Cave Men, which was very useful if you had a huge dead woolly elephant lying around

Famous Cave Men

There were no famous Cave Men. This is because newspapers and mags had not yet been invented

ANCIENT EGYPT

Chapter 2

a poem about Ancient Egypt

The statues in Egypt are rubbish

In spite of what everyone thinks

So I took out my hammer and chisel

And carved some huge boobs on the
Sphinx

History

Ancient Egypt was once just a huge pile of sand with lots of different tribes living on it

One day, all the tribes got together and instead of having a massive fight they decided to invent civilization

What Was Egypt Like?

If you were rich, living in Egypt was a bit like being a Hollywood movie star

If you were poor you had to go around with no clothes on grubbing through camel poo for something to eat

What Were Egyptians Like?

Looks

All Egyptians thought it was very fashionable to wear wigs, fake beards and masses of eyeliner

They also had a very peculiar style of walking

Pharaohs

The best job in Ancient Egypt by miles was being a Pharaoh. This meant you were unbelievably rich, you got to wear the trendiest clothes and absolutely everyone wanted to Do It with you

The problem was that it was quite difficult to become a pharaoh

What Did Egyptians Do?

The Egyptians spent their whole time building giant houses called Pyramids for dead people

When you got buried under one of these, you were always allowed to take your favourite things with you for the next world

When they weren't building pyramids, Egyptians loved sunbathing, making sand castles and getting pissed on homebrew

What Did Egyptians Believe in?

The Egyptians had loads and loads of gods. They even believed that their pharaohs were gods who switched on the sun every morning

Contributions to the World

The World would have been a very different place if the Egyptians had not invented the wheel

They also invented paper, pens and a special secret code for writing important messages in

The Egyptians made up strange and powerful curses for their tombs, which can still affect people today

Famous Egyptians

The most famous Egyptian was called Tutankhamen. His friends thought he was so smashing that they wrapped him in lav paper and buried him for 3000 years

Chapter 3

ANCIENT GREECE

a poem about
↓
Ancient Greece

The Spartans all hid in a huge wooden horse
Which everyone reckoned was fab
But what if you needed to rush to the lav
Cos you'd just had a dodgy kebab?

History

Once upon a time a god called Zeus turned himself into a bull and swam to Crete. His son invented Greece

The Greeks spent their whole time fighting each other. Their biggest war was called the Trojan War. It starred a sexy girl called Helen and a giant horse with men inside it.

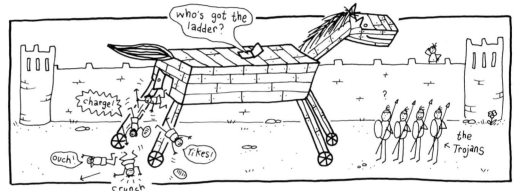

What was Greece Like?

The Greeks had some amazing cities. One bloke built a really smashing one called Atlantis but somehow he lost it

The Greeks kept all their stuff in pots and vases which had pictures of people Doing It all over them

What Were Greeks Like?

Looks

Greek men thought they were so handsome that all they should wear was sandals. Greek women wore dresses that showed their bosoms off well.

Greek Men

There were only 2 kinds of Greek men

All Greek men were completely sex mad. They Did It with anyone and anything they could find

Greek Women

Greek women were hardly allowed to do anything without their husbands' permission - not even go to the lav

What Did Greeks Do?

The Greeks spent a lot of their time making up incredibly long stories and poems to bore their friends with in the pub

The Greeks invented the Olympic Games which was really an excuse for a huge party with nudie running races

Every Greek person liked to have their own theory about something, however weird or nutty it might be

What Did Greeks Believe In?

As well as gods, the Greeks had things called Oracles which people used to go to for advice on important things

Contributions to the World

It was the Greeks who invented the 2 most disgusting drinks in the World

You needed to drink loads of this before you could eat their other most famous invention

Famous Greeks

Aristotle

Aristotle was the cleverest person in the world ever. He invented philosophy, logic, maths, physics, biology and mud-wrestling.

Archimedes

No-one knows exactly what Archimedes' Principle really was except that he thought of it while staring at his dangly bits in the bath

THE ROMANS

munch

← pizza

a poem about The Romans

Hanging out in Ancient Rome
Was really quite exciting
Cos when you weren't at orgies
You were getting pissed or fighting

History

In 753 B.C. a bloke called Romulus, whose Mum was a wolf, built a giant town on 7 hills.
He called it Rome

The Roman Empire became the most enormous power in the World. This was because they were very bossy and organised and they made their armies march for miles and miles

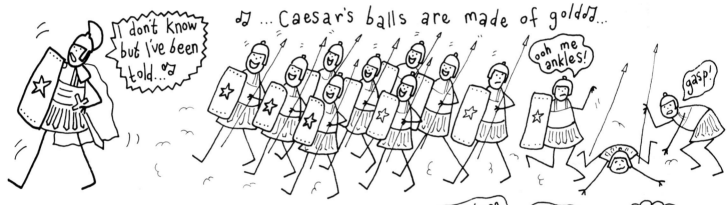

What was Rome Like

The main thing about Rome was the market places. These were a good place to buy slaves

Romans built masses of temples but they forgot to give them walls, so they were always chilly and fell down very quickly

What Were Romans Like?

Looks

Roman men had big crooked noses and bald patches. Roman women had long curly hair and bulging thighs

Roman Men

Roman men were very keen on wearing girls' clothes

They wore dresses for parties...

...and skirts when they went to war

Most Roman men had the same name, which could be quite confusing

Roman Women

Roman women usually stayed at home while eunuchs sung them songs

They were brilliant at making spaghetti and pizzas

What Did Romans Do?

Romans loved nothing better than getting into the bath with loads of mates and playing Hunt the Soap

Although people say Romans were civilised, their favourite thing was to watch gladiators chopping each other up, and christians being eaten by lions

Roman people used to go to the theatre a lot, but that was because no-one had invented the movies or T.V. yet

What Did Romans Believe In?

The Romans believed in a sort of gang of gods who used to spend their time playing tricks on people

Contributions to the World

By far the greatest contribution the Romans made to the world was inventing the orgy

The Romans also invented Latin which some people say is the greatest language in the world. But if it is so great why does no-one speak it anymore?

Although Romans had some quite clever ideas- they were not always the most interesting

Famous Romans

Julius Caesar

Julius Caesar was a power-crazed maniac who was done in by his best friend

Caligula

The main thing about Caligula was that he liked snogging horses

Chapter 5

ANCIENT CHINA

bow

a poem about

Ancient China

One of the cleverest bits of advice
That old chinese proverbs have said
Is "Man who tells girlfriend her bottom's
                                    too fat
Gets heavy thing thrown at his head"

History

Ages ago a huge gang of people built an enormous round wall. They called everything inside it China

shangs   Chous   Hans   Chins

Ancient China was ruled over by Dynasties, which was a posh Chinese way of saying families. Each Dynasty had a different style

Most Emperors of Ancient China got quite big-headed because they ruled over about a thousand million people

where's my personal bogie picker?

What was Ancient China Like?

The main thing about Ancient China was that it was very very very big

wow!

hover

China

rest of World

What Were the Chinese Like?

Looks

Ancient Chinese people liked wearing dressing gowns, funny hats and dangly beards and moustaches

They were very worried about how good they were in bed, so they kept making up special Make-you-Brilliant-at-Doing-It Potions

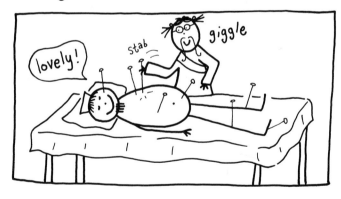

The Ancient Chinese used to relax by sticking loads of giant needles into each other

Chinese people loved animals

What Did the Chinese Do?

Ancient Chinese writing was so long and complicated that they hardly had any time to do anything else

When they weren't writing stuff, the Chinese liked to make up very peculiar stories about complete rubbish

What Did the Chinese Believe In?

Ancient Chinese people had a god for almost everything

Then some of them started to worship a giant fat man with big bosoms

And others started believing in all sorts of different stuff

Contributions to the World

Hardly anything in the world was invented that hadn't been thought up first by the Chinese. Here are a few of their cleverest inventions:-

Gunpowder

Tea

Printing

Spaghetti

Lav Paper

Pork Scratchings

Famous Ancient Chinese People

The most famous Ancient Chinese person was Confucius. No-one understood anything he said, but they all thought he was amazing anyway

THE VIKINGS

a poem about

The Vikings

The plundering pillaging Vikings
Were savage and cruel and unkind
The worst of their vices
Was munching thick slices
Of barbecued Briton's behind

History

The Vikings lived in a dark, freezing, rainy place where there was sometimes no sunshine for weeks

Because they spent so much time Doing It to keep warm there were soon too many Vikings in Viking Land so they set off to find new places to live

Vikings were brilliant at torturing, burning, killing, and smashing things up. This meant that they could live almost anywhere they wanted

A lot of Vikings came to England where they made loads more baby Vikings, but in the end they were chucked out by a Norman called William

What Were Vikings Like?

Looks

Vikings had flaky skin, ginger hair, straggly beards and smelly breath. The women were not very different

Viking Men

Viking men wore pointy hats which came in 2 styles-wings and horns

A Viking man was never ever allowed to show any signs of girliness

Viking Women

All Viking Women had to do was farming, housework, cooking, looking after loads of children, then snogging their husbands all night

What Did Vikings Do?

There was nothing a Viking loved more than a really good food fight

They also liked getting hold of all the latest gear. Sometimes they did this by trading, but usually they just stole things

What Did Vikings Believe In?

There were all sorts of groovy Viking gods One of the best was Thor, who was in charge of war, lightning and thunder

The head god was called Odin. He hung out in a huge palace where he partied with loads of dead warriors and sexy babes called Valkyries

Contributions to the World

The Vikings invented the World's weirdest funerals, where you were put in a ship with lots of dead animals and naked ladies. Then your mates all Did It with your wife, set fire to you and pushed you out to sea.

The silliest invention the Vikings ever made was Figure Skating

Famous Vikings

The most famous Viking was Leif Eriksson. He sailed all the way to America, but had to leave because he didn't like being teased by the Red Indians

Chapter 7

THE MIDDLE AGES

?

...durr

The Middle Ages

Merlin the Magician
Had some very groovy tricks
He could make his eyes go swirly
And see straight through ladies' knicks

History

There were loads of kings in the Middle Ages all with the same names. Only one of them was called Stephen

English men in the Middle Ages spent 100 years trying to kill French men. This was mainly because English men thought French girls were more sexy than English girls

When they got bored the English people decided to fight each other but they didn't use swords- they hit each other with flowers instead

Most people in the Middle Ages died of the Plague. You knew you had the Plague if you sneezed and then went black and died

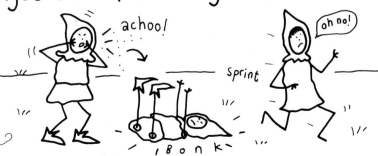

What Were the Middle Ages Like?

In the Middle Ages rich people owned all the land and poor people had to do all their work for them

There were no lavs in the Middle Ages so everyone used to throw their poo straight out of the window

Wherever you went in the Middle Ages, there were always loads of people with strange diseases and bits dropping off them

Instead of going to the pub young men used to spend their time slaying dragons and rescuing sexy maidens from towers

What Did People Do In the Middle Ages?

Knights - One of the best jobs in the Middle Ages was being a knight.

Great Things about being a Knight:-

You could wear a special outfit that stopped you from ever being killed in battles

You could put on pretend fights with your mates to make all the ladies fancy you

You got to go on loads of foreign holidays

Witches - There were loads of witches around in the Middle Ages

Good Things about being a Witch	Bad Things about being a Witch
You could wear a pointy hat and make up weird spells	lots of people liked killing Witches

Contributions to the World

Most people in the Middle Ages were very stupid so they hardly invented anything at all

But they did manage to make up a game called Football.

And it was some time in the Middle Ages that the Chastity Belt was invented

SPRING COLLECTION

fabulous

perfect!

jingle

Famous People in the Middle Ages

Chaucer

Chaucer wrote an incredibly long story about lots of people Doing It with each other

chaucer

rubbish spelling

canter-burie-taulies

Robin Hood

Even though Robin Hood wore tights and liked nicking stuff everyone thought he was a hero

stash

We love you

Chapter 8

THE AZTECS

a poem about

The Aztecs

The fierce and bloodthirsty Aztecs

Had all sorts of ways to have fun

Like if you got stuck

And you needed good luck

You could go home and chop up your

Mum

History

At first the Aztecs were a poor homeless tribe who wandered around Mexico looking for somewhere to live

But soon they had built an enormous floating city with massive temples and palaces covered with gold and jewels

Then some Spaniards came along who the Aztecs thought were gods because they had not seen anyone like them before

Eventually the Spaniards were rumbled so they killed all the Aztecs and completely destroyed their city. That was the end of the Aztecs

What Were Aztecs Like?

Looks

Aztecs were short people with dark skins who all had the same hairstyle

Aztecs were very keen on:-

body-piercing

tattoos

Jewellery

Aztec Men

Aztec men loved dressing up in bows, feathers and animal costumes - especially when they went into battle

Aztec Women

Aztec women liked painting groovy patterns all over their privates

What Did Aztecs Do?

The Aztecs spent most of their time sucking up to their gods by making hundreds of human sacrifices

They were also very fond of eating each other. Arms and legs were the tastiest bits. Tummies, bottoms and doodahs were thrown to the animals

When it came to building their cities, Aztecs liked to use the heads of their enemies for making the walls with

What Did Aztecs Believe In?

The Aztecs had some quite strange gods, one of them was a bundle of talking rubbish in a magic box

Another was a Lady god who gave birth to the moon and stars

Contributions to the World

The Aztecs built amazing floating gardens where they grew their vegetables, but because they didn't have many animals, they used their own poo as fertilizer

Aztecs were not allowed to drink booze, so they spent their whole time making up all sorts of drugs out of whatever they could find

Their worst invention was a small hairless dog for old ladies called the Chihuahua

Famous Aztecs

The most famous Aztec was called Montezuma. Anyone who disobeyed him got cursed with a runny bottom which lasted for ages

THE TUDORS

cheers!

a poem about

The Tudors

The Tudors invented the codpiece
Which laced up the middle with strings
Some men would stuff giant marrows
inside
So girlies would gasp at their Things

History

Kings and Queens

The most important Tudor king was Henry VIII. He was famous for:-

1. Not being very nice to his wives

2. Being unbelievably fat

The most important Queen was Elizabeth I. She was famous for never Doing It with anyone _ever_

The main thing about Tudor history is that England, France and Spain spent the whole time trying to blow each other up

It was in Tudor times that everyone in England started to build houses that looked like pubs

What Were Tudors Like?

People in Tudor times used to spend all the money they had on clothes

Tudor Men

Tudor Men liked wearing girly hats, fishnet stockings and furry willy covers

Tudor Women

Tudor Women wore giant frames under their skirts. This made it very easy to hide your secret lovers...

...but very difficult to get undressed in a hurry

What Did Tudors Do?

Tudors spent most of their time in Ale Houses, where you could get completely pissed, throw stuff at people and Do It with rude ladies

When they weren't at Ale Houses, Tudors loved to have their mates round for massive feasts

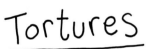

Tortures

Tudors loved nothing more than a good bit of torture. Here are some of the best ones

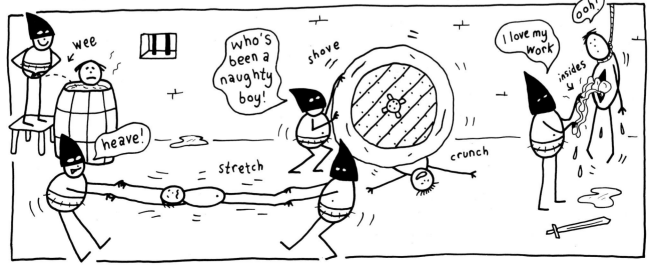

Contributions to the World

It was the Tudors who invented the toilet and discovered potatoes and tobacco

Probably the most useless invention the Tudors made was the ruff. This was a giant frilly collar-type thing which even men liked wearing

Famous People from Tudor Times

Shakespeare

William Shakespeare wrote plays about history and comedies with no jokes in them

One of the people in his plays was called Bottom

Columbus

Christopher Columbus was the man who discovered America

Chapter 10

THE VICTORIANS

stroll

a poem about ↓ The Victorians

"Children, my dear, should be seen and not heard"
Victorians all liked to say
So they gave them a helping of mouldy rat stew
And then stuffed them up chimneys all day

History

In Victorian times the English thought they were amazing, and went around trying to take over most of the world

At home there was a thing called the Industrial Revolution. This meant that instead of working with their hands people had to find out how to use machines

What Were Victorian Times Like?

In Victorian England everything got covered with loads of frills and fancy bits

All Victorians thought that discipline was a very good thing

What Were Victorians Like?

Victorian Men

Victorian Men liked wearing top hats, sideburns, whiskers and frock coats to try to make themselves look posh

Victorian Women

Victorian Women wore huge lacy undies and tiny corsets to make themselves look skinnier than they were

Victorian people pretended that Doing It was too rude to exist and that even a tiny peep of skin was the naughtiest thing in the world

But in secret they used to sneak off to Saucy Clubs and do all sorts of things with everyone in sight

What Did Victorians Do?

Posh Victorians spent a lot of time being polite and dainty and drinking cups of tea with each other

Poor Victorians had to do all the work. Even their children were made to go out and earn a living

Because so many people were poor, there were loads of thieves around

Victorian Holidays

Victorians loved the seaside but they went to great lengths to stop people from seeing their privates

Contributions to the World

The Victorians made a lot of amazing inventions. Here are some of the best :-

1. Electricity

2. The Gramophone

3. The Steam Train

4. The Tea Cosy

Famous Victorians

By miles the most famous Victorian was Queen Victoria

Things we know about Queen Victoria

She ruled for an incredibly long time

She never understood anyone's jokes

There was also a writer called Charles Dickens. His books were so long most people had to wait till the T.V. was invented to find out what they were about

Chapter 11

THE 20th CENTURY

a poem about ↓

The 20th Century

I sometimes get asked "What achievements
Did the 20th Century see?"
But I just shrug my shoulders
                    politely
And carry on watching T.V.

History

The two most horrible wars ever were fought in the 20th Century

The first one was against the Germans

The second one was against the Germans too

The main stars of the Second World War were:-

1. Winston Churchill

He was a chubby Englishman with big cigars

2. Adolf Hitler

He was a crazy German with a silly moustache

After the 2 World Wars came the Cold War which the communists lost. This meant that everyone in the world could enjoy burgers and fizzy drinks

Because T.V. was invented in the 20th Century, countries began to elect their leaders on how handsome they were rather than how clever they were.

What Was the 20th Century Like?

Everyone in the 20th Century was in a hurry, so people started making things that could do everything quicker.

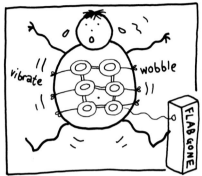

It was the 20th Century when women all over the world began to get more and more powerful

Half way through the 20th Century teenagers were invented. These were people with spots and squeaky voices who were allowed to be rude to their parents

All sorts of new drugs came about in the 20th Century which made people behave in lots of different ways

What Did 20th Century People Do?

There were 2 main things that people did in the 20th Century

WORK-which was boring and SHOPPING-which was fun

Some very clever people decided that a good way of making lots of money was to invent a thing called Modern Art

Fashions changed a lot in the 20th Century. Here are some of the best ones

What Did 20th Century People Believe In?

The main thing that people worshipped in the 20th Century was Pop Stars. When they went to see their favourite Pop Stars everyone used to scream and faint and throw their pants at them

Contributions to the World

By miles the most important invention in the world was T.V. This meant that no-one ever had to be bored again

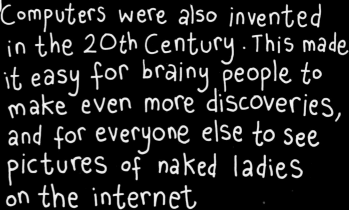

Computers were also invented in the 20th Century. This made it easy for brainy people to make even more discoveries, and for everyone else to see pictures of naked ladies on the internet

One of the best discoveries of the 20th Century was cloning. Cloning was very useful if you wanted to make a hippo-donkey-fish

Famous 20th Century People

Elvis Presley

He was a fat man who sang songs and died on the lav eating burgers

Princess Di

She was a skinny lady with some dodgy boyfriends who everyone thought was smashing

whizz ← the World

THE END

Also by Purple Ronnie

Purple Ronnies Little Poems for Friends

Purple Ronnies Little Guide to Boyfriends

Purple Ronnies Little Book of Willies and Bottoms

Purple Ronnie's Little Guide for Lovers